THIS BOOK BELONGS TO:

_____

_____

_____

I like tea!

I prefer coffee!

I collect pine cones.

I play the banjo.

Bat rays are cute.

Axolotls are neat.

meomi

This book was written and illustrated by MEOMI
(the not-secret pen name of Vicki Wong & Michael Murphy).
Learn more about them at www.meomi.com

OTHER BOOKS BY MEOMI:
The Octonauts & the Only Lonely Monster
The Octonauts & the Sea of Shade
The Octonauts & the Frown Fish
The Octonauts & the Great Ghost Reef

First published in hardback in Great Britain by HarperCollins Children's Books in 2012
First published in paperback in 2013

9 10 8

ISBN: 978-0-00-828330-8

HarperCollins Children's Books is a division of HarperCollins Publishers Ltd.

Text and illustrations copyright © MEOMI Design Inc.:
Vicki Wong and Michael Murphy 2012, 2013

Visit our website at: www.harpercollins.co.uk

Printed and bound in China by RR Donnelley APS

KWAZII PESO BARNACLES INKLING KWAZII

TUNIP TWEAK DASHI SHELLINGTON

PESO BARNACLES INKLING KWAZII PESO

TWEAK TUNIP

BARNACLES BARNACLES

DASHI TWEAK

INKLING INKLING

THE OCTONAUTS

Beep
Beep

Explore the Great Big Ocean

· MEOMI ·

HarperCollins *Children's Books*

It was a busy day under the cold Arctic Ocean when...

Captain Barnacles bear was doing his laundry.

Tweak bunny was clearing ice in the GUP-D.

Dashi dog was updating the Octopod's software.

Peso penguin was practising his bandaging.

OCTO-OS 8
INSERT DISK 4 (OF
READY.

ALERT! ALERT!

Kwazii kitten was working on his cat fu.

Professor Inkling octopus was leading a game.

Shellington sea otter was researching with...

...Tunip the Vegimal, who had just sounded the Octo-alert!

DUNGEON MODULE 01
Oceans & Ogres

Sliding through chutes and climbing down ladders,
the rest of the Octonauts hurried to the launch bay.
There they found Tunip anxiously pointing to
a large map on the screen.

"Bree dakoo wook," he chirped sadly.

"We were studying underwater biomes,"
Shellington explained. "Every creature has a home –
a special place called a 'habitat' – that provides shelter and food.
Tunip is upset because he doesn't know
which habitat Vegimals belong to!"

"Where did the Vegimals come from?" Peso asked.

"That's a good question!" Shellington said as he began to read from his journal.

One day, while doing research outside, I noticed some strange shapes on the side of the Octopod.

They looked like giant fish eggs, but unlike any I'd seen before!

It was too dangerous to leave them outside...

so I brought them into my lab.

After a few days, the eggs hatched...

...and that's how I discovered the

Vegimals!

MY VEGIMAL JOURNAL

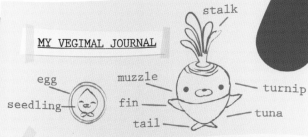

egg · seedling · muzzle · stalk · fin · tail · turnip · tuna

Day 1: There are dozens of them - little creatures that appear to be half-vegetable and half-animal! I took it upon myself to give them appropriate names.

Tunip
F:Tuna
V:Turnip

Sharchini
F:Shark
V:Zucchini
(Courgette)

Perchkin
F:Perch
V:Pumpkin

Halibeet
F:Halibut
V:Beet

Day 5: They communicate through a sophisticated language of chirps and warbles that I haven't quite deciphered,eg: "Cheepa" "Dakko doo"

Yamchovy
FV:Yam
F:Anchovy

Wallabaga
F:Walleye
V:Rutabaga
(Swede)

Pikato
F:Pike
V:Tomato

Charchard
F:Char
V:Chard

Day 12: They seem to have designated the Vegimal 'TUNIP' as their spokesperson.
*Note to self: Look into hive-mind behaviours.

Maccoli
F:Mackerel
V:Broccoli

Carprika
F:Carp
V:Paprika

Albachoy
F:Albacore
V:Bok Choy

Salpeno
F:Salmon
V:Jalapeño

Day 26: The Vegimals have left the lab and become an essential part of day-to-day operations on the Octopod! They're especially fond of kelp and have taken to the kitchen & garden pod.

I don't know where the eggs came from or how long they'd been attached to our ship – they could be from anywhere in the ocean!

Captain Barnacles declared,

OCTONAUTS!

Our mission is to visit the different habitats of the ocean and find where Vegimals come from! Prepare the GUPs!

Compass

Telescope

Magnifying glass

Medical kit

Stethoscope

Maps

Pencil and paper

Bandages

Extra sock

Air tanks

Cameras

Guide books

Kelp cakes

Hammer

Screwdriver

Deep-sea diving suits

Toolbox

Wrench

More kelp cakes

The team worked together to pack their tools and equipment, while the Vegimals made sure there were plenty of their favourite kelp cakes to eat for the long trip ahead.

GUP-C

GUP-E

GUP-B

Generator

Floodlight

Air tanks

Research
computer

Dorsal
stabiliser

Bubble engine

Cargo hold

Bunbot

Navigation
computer

Stowaway

Secret storage

GUP-A

GUP-D

One by one, the GUPs launched from the Octopod!

First, the Octonauts visited the bustling **OPEN OCEAN**.
Amongst the waves, they met wandering sunfish,
migrating whales and a boisterous giant squid.
Tunip was impressed that some creatures
lived their entire lives on the move!

Scallop

Conch

Pen shell

Limpet

Banded tulip

Shells make great homes!

On the rocky **BEACH**, the Octonauts were invited to a tide pool party.
Tunip discovered that many creatures live in shells.
Unfortunately, they were too small to be Vegimal homes!

COWFISH CORRAL

Moo

MANATEE FARMS

In the **SEAGRASS MEADOWS**, the Octonauts helped
the gentle manatee farmers with their harvest.
Shellington discovered many baby animals
in the nursery but none of them were Vegimals.

NURSERY

Let's take a
closer look!

CRABS

HOGFISH

SEAGRASS WRASSE

GOATFISH

PIPEFISH

When the Octonauts reached
the sunny **CORAL REEF**, they were
dazzled by the bright colours.
Friendly sea slugs, perched on giant
sponges, greeted them at every turn.
But wherever they looked,
every burrow and nook was already home
to a creature. There wasn't any room
left for the Vegimals!

I'm a
surgeon...
fish!

I'm a
medic!

In the murky **SWAMP**, the Octonauts nervously drifted past grinning alligators and curious snakes.

Bonjour

WELCOME

Under the water, they discovered a parade! The crew
danced through the bayou while the Vegimals collected
beads as souvenirs. Tired out from all the merrymaking,
Tunip decided they should continue their search.

After a long descent, the Octonauts reached the bottom of the ocean to visit their **DEEP SEA** research lab. The crew inspected the camera network but they didn't see any Vegimals, only the flickering lights of bioluminescent jellyfish.

Turn off the lights and see me glow!

Octobuggy

Seismograph

Light tower

Tulip gazed out at the smoky hydrothermal vents
and felt like he was on a different planet.
He wondered if he'd *ever* find his own habitat.

Deep-sea network

OCTOLAB

Camera

Octobot

When the Octonauts finally arrived at the **KELP FOREST**, Tunip's eyes widened and he clapped his fins together in delight. Everywhere he looked, he was surrounded by kelp, his favourite type of seaweed.

"There aren't any other Vegimals here," Shellington observed.
"But it appears to be a suitable habitat for them...
Vegimals do love kelp!"

The Vegimals quickly set up a camp kitchen and began baking away!
They made sweet chocolate kelp cakes, healthy broccoli kelp cakes,
and even fancy pineapple upside-down kelp cakes!

MENU DE KELP

Classic kelp

Apple

Cupcake

Chocolate

Miso

Neapolitan

Watermelon

Burger

Peppermint

Pancake

Cactus

Swiss cheese

Strawberry

Sauerkraut

Pickle

Onion

Licorice

Mushroom

Broccoli

Kimchi

Jelly

Candy floss

Cappuccino

Pumpkin

Kiwi

Lemon

Pineapple

When it was time to leave,
Shellington called out, "Tunip, are you ready to go?"
But the distracted Vegimals were too busy to respond.

"Looks like they want to stay here,"
Captain Barnacles said sadly.
"I guess our search is over and
we should head home
to the Octopod."

Roll Blend Bake

Fold Ice Churn Whisk Stir mix

Glaze

The Octonauts waved farewell as they departed in their GUPs,
while the Vegimals continued to work in a fervour.
So much kelp, so many cakes to bake!

The Vegimals rolled and mixed and stirred for days – until mountains of kelp cakes towered all around them. With the baking done, Tunip excitedly ran through the forest in search of the Octonauts. He couldn't wait to share these treats.

Not finding a single crew member, Tunip finally remembered – they had all gone back to the Octopod!

There was no one left to enjoy the cakes.

Missing their friends, the gloomy Vegimals thought of all the fun times they'd had together and felt sad.

The Vegimals didn't know where the Octopod would be,
but they all agreed they had to try and find it.

With a long and difficult journey ahead of them,
they quickly packed up their mobile kitchen.
Plates were stacked and pots were stowed.
The determined group left the forest in a jumble
of carts spilling with cakes.

They travelled back to all the different habitats they'd visited, from the busy open ocean to the deep sea floor.

As days passed, the Vegimals grew tired and
started to give up hope of ever finding the Octonauts.
Until suddenly one morning, they heard a familiar sound…

VROoooOM

The Octopod! The Vegimals cheered as it landed beside them in a burst of bubbles. The Octohatch promptly opened and the Octonauts swam out to reunite with their friends.

"We missed you all so much!" Captain Barnacles said as he gave Tunip a big bear hug. "We returned to the kelp forest to visit... but you weren't there!"

"Luckily, we found a trail of delicious clues!" Dashi added,
as each Octonaut held up their favourite type of cake.

Yarrrgh!
How did I get
licorice again?!!

"The Octopod hasn't been the same without you!"
Barnacles addressed all the Vegimals.
"Would you join us on board again?"

"CHEEPA CHOO!!" Tunip quickly replied.

The crew all turned expectedly to Shellington,
who explained with a grin, "That's Vegimalese for 'YES'!!"

Back on board the ship, the Octonauts gathered
in the garden pod to enjoy a picnic.

"Tunip, if you like, we can keep looking for your original habitat?"
Shellington said in between mouthfuls of kelp cake.
"There's still so much ocean we've yet to explore..."

Tunip looked around at his caring friends and cheerfully
shook his head. He knew there was no better place
for a Vegimal to belong than right here –
on the **OCTOPOD!**

THE END

THE OCTONAUTS: MEET THE CREW!

CAPTAIN BARNACLES BEAR

Captain Barnacles is a brave polar bear extraordinaire and the leader of the Octonauts crew. He's always the first to rush in and help whenever there's a problem. In addition to exploring, Barnacles enjoys playing his accordion and writing in his captain's log.

KWAZII KITTEN

Kwazii is a daredevil orange kitten with a mysterious pirate past. He's never one to turn down an adventure and he loves travelling to exotic places. His favourite hobbies include long baths, racing the GUP-B, and general swashbuckling.

PESO PENGUIN

Peso is the medic for the team. He's an expert at bandaging and always carries his medical kit with him in case of emergencies. He's not too fond of scary things, but if a creature is hurt or in danger, Peso can be the bravest Octonaut of all!

DASHI DOG

Dashi is a sweet dachshund who oversees operations in the Octopod HQ and launch bay. She monitors the computers and manages all ship traffic. She's also the Octonauts' official photographer and enjoys taking photos of undersea life.

TWEAK BUNNY

Tweak is the engineer for the Octopod. She keeps everything working in the launch bay and maintains the Octonauts' GUPs. Tweak enjoys tinkering and inventing strange machines that sometimes work in unexpected ways.

PROFESSOR INKLING OCTOPUS

Professor Inkling is a brilliant Dumbo octopus oceanographer. He founded the Octonauts with the intention of furthering underwater research and preservation. Because of his delicate, big brain, he prefers to help the team from his library in the Octopod.

DR SHELLINGTON SEA OTTER

Dr Shellington is a nerdy sea otter scientist who loves doing field research and working in his lab. He's easily distracted by rare plants and animals, but his knowledge of the ocean is a big help in Octonaut missions.

TUNIP THE VEGIMAL

Tunip is one of many Vegimals; special sea creatures that are part vegetable and part animal. They speak their own language that only Shellington can understand (sometimes!) Vegimals help out around the Octopod and love to bake: kelp cakes, kelp cookies, kelp soufflé...